TO ALL THE BUSY LITTLE COWPOKES
I KNOW AND HAVE YET TO MEET.
I LOVE YOU, AND I AIN'T KIDDIN'
ABOUT THAT! YEE HA!
— S.G.F.

TO MY NIECES JESSICA,
CAMMIE, AND SADIE
— R.C.

First edition 2019

Published by Peter Pauper Press, Inc.
202 Mamaroneck Avenue
White Plains, New York 10601 USA

Library of Congress Cataloging-in-Publication Data

Names: Fortson, Sarah Glenn, author. | Cox, Russ, illustrator.
Title: This cowgirl ain't kiddin' about the potty / by Sarah Glenn Fortson ;
illustrated by Russ Cox.
Other titles: This cowgirl is not kidding about the potty
Description: First edition. | White Plains, New York : Peter Pauper Press,
Inc., 2019. | Summary: Cowgirl A.K. saunters about in her ten-gallon hat
and two-quart diaper, insisting she has no time for the potty, until she
meets her idol, Wild Wilma Wilkee, who wears underwear.
Identifiers: LCCN 2019003014 | ISBN 9781441331656 (hardcover : alk. paper)
Subjects: | CYAC: Cowgirls--Fiction. | Toilet training--Fiction. |
Determination (Personality trait)--Fiction. | Humorous stories.
Classification: LCC PZ7.1.F668 Thi 2019 | DDC [E]--dc23 LC record available at https://lccn.loc.gov/2019003014

ISBN 978-1-4413-3165-6
Manufactured for Peter Pauper Press, Inc.
Printed in Hong Kong

7 6 5 4 3 2 1

Visit us at www.peterpauper.com

THIS COWGIRL AIN'T KIDDIN' ABOUT THE POTTY

BY SARAH GLENN FORTSON
ILLUSTRATED BY RUSS COX

PETER PAUPER PRESS, INC.
White Plains, New York

"BREAKFAST!"

Cowgirl A.K. sauntered into the kitchen, wearing her ten-gallon hat and her two-quart diaper.

IT WAS CHOW TIME.

"**HOLD IT RIGHT THERE, MISSY.**

Didn't we say no diapers today?"

"Ma'am, **I'M A COWGIRL**.
I've got fences to varnish,
horses to harness,
and spurs that tarnish.

Ain't kiddin'.
I got no time for the potty."

SCHOOL TRIP
Tasso's

"BRRRiiiiNG!"

Cowgirl A.K. strolled down the hallway wearing her ten-gallon hat and her two-quart diaper.

IT WAS LEARNIN' TIME.

"Well, mornin', A.K.
WHOA NOW, what's that?
A diaper under those jeans?"

"Sir, **I'M A COWGIRL**.
I've got fences to varnish,
horses to harness,
and spurs that tarnish.

Ain't kiddin'.
I got no time for the potty."

COW
RODE

After lunch the other kids made
their way to the bathroom.
A.K. paid them no mind.

IT WAS STUDYIN' TIME.

She read about broncobusters,
barrel racers, and bull riders.

Teacher said, "Tomorrow we're going to a wrangling rodeo where we'll see the most famous cowgirl of all, Wild Wilma Wilkee."

That night A.K. chose her outfit for the big day.

"Cowgirls can't be late for rodeos. **AIN'T KIDDIN'**."

Next day, A.K. was a
cracklin' and a hummin',
with her ten-gallon hat,
set just right,

her tall red boots,
polished nice 'n' bright.

And in her new denim jeans—
she was quite a sight.

After the barrel racers and bull riders,
finally, it was Wild Wilma time.
She rode out on one of the
baddest broncos ever!

But Wilma never let go.

Wild Wilma finished with a bow and
a wave of her hat.
"**YEE HA!** And good night!"

A.K. followed Wilma through the crowds, hoping for an autograph.

She kept her eyes on Wilma's tall red boots, until all of a sudden . . .

. . . the boots disappeared.

A.K. looked left. A.K. looked right.

Wild Wilma had vanished.

Then a potty door opened . . . out stepped one red boot, then two.

It was Wild Wilma!

Wild
Wilma

Wilma looked at A.K. "Howdy-do, that's a fine ten-gallon hat you're wearing. Would you like me to sign it?"

"**YESSIREE**! That would be mighty nice. And Ma'am, could we get a picture?"

Back at the bunkhouse,
the day was winding down.

A.K. placed her new photo
beside her bed and took
ONE MORE LOOK.

Wild Wilma

WILMA HAD . . .

A ten-gallon hat set just right.
Tall red boots, polished nice 'n' bright.
And denim jeans—she was quite a sight.

COWGIRL A.K. HAD . . .

A ten-gallon hat set just right.
Tall red boots, polished nice 'n' bright.
And denim jeans, . . .

UH-OH!

with diaper fringe in sight.

Wild Wilma

She checked pictures of Wild Wilma again.

"THAT'S IT!" said A.K.

"Wild Wilma doesn't wear diapers. She wears underwear!"

A.K. yanked off her left boot.

Wild Wilma

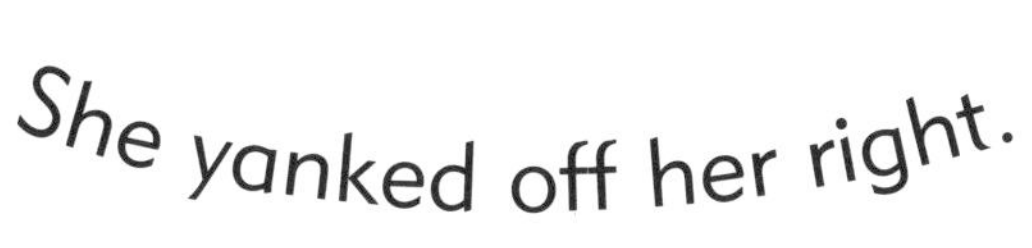

She yanked off her right.

She shimmied out of her jeans,

and whipped off her diaper.

Prancing proud in a brand-new pair
of bronco-bustin' undies,
A.K. hollered,

"RIDE 'EM COWGIRL!"

and galloped down the hall.

IT WAS POTTY TIME.

Wild

The cowgirl eyed that big white stallion.
She knew what to do.

BOOM!

WHOOSH! GURGLE! GURGLE! GROAN.

A.K. took a bow, waved her (autographed) hat, and hollered,

"YEE HA! And good night."

Mom said, "Finally A.K.! You're serious about this underwear thing, right?"

"Ma'am, **I'M A COWGIRL**. I've got fences to varnish, horses to harness, and spurs that tarnish."

"AIN'T KIDDIN' . . .

. . . I GOT NO TIME FOR DIAPERS."